POOH AND THE HONEY TREE

Winnie-the-Pooh had a very Important Time every day around about eleven o'clock when it was TIM FOUR A LITEL SUMHTING. And the Little Something was usually honey. But this particular morning there was nothing left in any of the honey pots! While he was thinking what to do he heard a buzzing and buzzing means bees which means honey, and that is how Pooh found the honey tree.

Other titles in this series:

WINNIE-THE-POOH AND TIGGER TOO
POOH AND PIGLET GO HUNTING
WINNIE-THE-POOH AND THE BLUSTERY DAY
POOH IN A TIGHT PLACE

Scholastic Book Services Inc.,
10 Earlham Street, London WC2H 9LN

Scholastic Inc.,
730 Broadway, New York, NY 10003, USA

Scholastic Tab Publications Ltd.,
123 Newkirk Road, Richmond Hill,
Ontario L4C 3G5, Canada

Ashton Scholastic Pty. Ltd., Box 579, Gosford,
New South Wales, Australia

Ashton Scholastic Ltd., 165 Marua Road,
Panmure, Auckland, New Zealand

First published in West Germany by Ravensburger Taschenbücher, 1983
First published in the UK by Scholastic Book Services Inc. 1985
Illustrations copyright © Walt Disney, 1983
This translation copyright © Scholastic Book Services Inc, 1985
Translated by Anthea Bell
Original Title *Puuh und der Honigbaum*
ISBN 0 590 70410 9

Made and printed in Spain by
Printer industria gráfica s.a. Barcelona
D.L.B. 2934-1985

POOH AND THE HONEY TREE

Translated by Anthea Bell

Hippo Books
Scholastic Book Services
London

My Friend Pooh

"Hallo, Pooh Bear!" I said. "I've been waiting for you."

"Hallo there!" said Winnie-the-Pooh.

Winnie-the-Pooh came walking along, waddling slightly because his legs are so short. I've known Pooh for years and years. I must have known him for at least fifty years!

We used to share a room. I mean, Pooh and some other friends of mine lived with me. You'll meet my other friends soon. Grown-ups said they were only stuffed toy animals, but that's not true. We lived in a wonderful, magic place called Hundred Acre Wood, which was part of the Forest, and of course it was a *real* Forest.

Winnie-the-Pooh lived in the Forest under the name of Sanders. It was up over his door in gold letters, so naturally he lived under it. There was another notice up on his door too. It said:

RNIG ALSO

He meant that you could ring his bell and then just walk in.
Winnie-the-Pooh was a very friendly bear.
I don't know exactly *why* he lived under the name of Sanders. Nobody in the Forest actually called him Sanders. But he had a lot of other names. Besides just Pooh, he could be called Winnie, Winnie-the-Pooh, or Pooh Bear. Another thing I don't know is who thought of calling him Winnie. It may have been an idea of Piglet's. Or perhaps Eeyore thought of it. Anyway, his own, real name was Pooh. He used to say his name out loud when he played his favourite game of blowing dandelion clocks. Try it yourself! Hold a dandelion clock in front

of your mouth and say, "Pooh!" You'll blow all
the seeds away.

And if a butterfly settled on Pooh's nose, and it
tickled him, he could say his own name, "Pooh!"
and blow it off again.

So perhaps that's why he was called Pooh.

Pooh and the Little Something

Pooh had a very Important Time every day, not long after he'd got up, round about eleven o'clock in the morning.

It was elevenses time. Or time for a little something, as Pooh called it. Not that he told everybody about it, only you and me. If he had to write it down, it came out like this:

TIM FOUR A LITELSUMHTING

Only as his name for it was a secret, he never *did* write it down.

It was elevenses, or time for a little something, or honey time. Bears are always hungry, and they will eat almost anything, but what they like best of all is honey.

Pooh had lots of pots of honey. But he liked honey so much that the pots soon got empty. Pooh was very thorough, and he liked to get to the bottom of things, particularly honey pots.

"Oh dear!" said Pooh, sadly. "Empty again! Just a little bit of stickiness round the rim!"

Greedy old Pooh had eaten so much honey that he was getting quite fat.

One day Pooh burst at the seams! Well, one seam burst anyway, the one down his back.

"Silly old Bear!" I said. "You'll have to get a bit thinner."

"Oh dear!" said Winnie-the-Pooh. "Christopher Robin, please would you get a needle and thread and sew me up again? My stuffing is all coming out."

"I'm afraid I'm not much good at sewing," I told him.

"But it doesn't look very nice, does it?" said Pooh. "All that fluff and stuff coming out! Please, Christopher Robin!"

I couldn't really say no, when Pooh Bear asked me so nicely, so I put a few stitches in him. I thought they'd hold him together a bit longer.

Bears are not particularly clever, but when Pooh really tried thinking, he thought very hard indeed. When he heard a clock strike, for instance, he knew that meant it was time for something.

"Can you think what it was I wanted to think

about now?" Pooh asked himself. And he told himself, "No, nor can I!"

"Think, think, think . . . oh, I know! It's time for my Stoutness Exercises," said Pooh.

So he did his Stoutness Exercises, and he made up a little hum to go with them. The words went like this:

"Up, down,
Touch the ground!
When I go up, down,
And touch the ground,
It puts me in the mood
for food!"

"Oh dear!" said Pooh to himself. "It's all rumbly in my tummy! I do believe it's time for elevenses! Time for a little something!"
And he went on humming happily to himself.

"I am short and fat,
And proud of that!
I am stout and round,
And I have found,
When I've a happy, happy appetite,
I'm a happy, happy Pooh!
Up, down,
Touch the ground!

When I go up, down,
And touch the ground
It puts me in the mood
For food."

And then Pooh's Poohcoo clock struck again,
just to remind him it really *was* time for a little
something, so he stopped humming in rather a
hurry.
Silly old, greedy old Pooh!

15

Pooh's New Words

I've told you about Pooh's Poohcoo clock, and
the way he blew dandelion clocks by saying his
own name.

He could make up other words with his name in
them too. For instance, if it was cold he wore a
Poohllover. And of course he washed his fur with
Shampooh. And sometimes, on a rainy day, he
liked to stay at home and do a jigsaw Poohzle.

If Pooh ever met a dog, he was pleased if it was a
poohdle. And he thought that if he had a cat, he
would call it Poohssy.

But sometimes he cheated, and put his name into
words where it wasn't really there at all. For
instance, he might tell you it was a poohtiful day.
His favourite sort of book, if only he'd been
better at reading, would have been a poohkery
book, because he was so fond of things to eat.
And he made up new sayings as well. *You* might
say somebody was hungry as a hunter, but Pooh
would say "hungry as a Pooh", and that meant
very hungry indeed. Hungry enough to eat a
whole pot of honey at once. Or if he said, "The

poohst of friends!" he meant the best of friends:
the kind a bear really likes to have.
Such as Piglet. Piglet really was Pooh's poohst
friend.
I'll tell you more about Piglet later.

Pooh Has a Think
Pooh was getting very, very thoughtful about
something again.
"Think, think, think," said Pooh to himself.
"Now, what *was* I trying to think of?"

While Pooh was thinking, he suddenly heard the sound of buzzing.

"That buzzing means something!" said Pooh. "I know what it means! Buzzing means bees!"

Now Pooh knew what he was trying to think of.

"And bees mean honey," said Pooh to himself. "And why do bees make honey? So that I can eat it!"

So Pooh climbed the honey tree, and on his way he sang a little song to himself.

"Isn't it funny
How a bear likes honey?
Buzz! Buzz! Buzz!
I wonder why he does?"

"Oh," said Pooh to himself, "my tummy's all rumbly inside! I don't know *why*, but I *do* like honey!"
Careful, Pooh Bear! You'd better watch out or. . .

"Oh help!" said Pooh to himself. "If only I
hadn't climbed this tree, I wouldn't have. . .this
is what comes of liking honey so much. Oh
help!" said Pooh, bouncing from branch to
branch, and finally he fell off the last branch and
landed in a gorse bush.

Pooh crawled out of the gorse bush, took the
prickles out of his fur, and asked the bush
crossly, "Why can't you go and grow somewhere
else?"

Pooh didn't often get cross, but anyone can see
why he felt cross now!

Pooh Needs Help

Christopher Robin lived in the Forest quite near his friends, so that he could help them if they ever needed anything.

There were lots of things Christopher Robin was going to do that fine summer's day. He was planning to mend his bicycle and tidy up his toys. Then he was going to play games with his friends in the clearing in the middle of the Hundred Acre Wood.

"Good morning, Christopher Robin," said Pooh, unhappily.

"Good morning, Pooh Bear," said Christopher Robin.

"If it *is* a good morning," growled Pooh, and he looked all round him.

"Looking for anything in particular, Pooh?" asked Christopher Robin.

"Well," said Pooh, "I *was* wondering if you had such a thing as a balloon about you."

"Well, yes, I have!" said Christopher Robin. "But what do you want a balloon for, Pooh?"

"Ssh!" said Pooh, in a loud whisper. And then he

added, "Honey!"

"But Pooh," said Christopher Robin, "you don't get honey with balloons!"

"I do, Christopher Robin!" said Pooh.

"How?" asked Christopher Robin.

"I fly up to the honey tree like a bee," said Pooh. "Look, like this!" And he took off. Christopher Robin was just in time to catch him.

"Wait a minute, Pooh! Don't be in such a hurry. The bees are sure to notice you."

"Not if I'm in disguise!" said Pooh. "Would you take me to the nice muddy place, and then I can splash around in it?"

So Christopher Robin took Winnie-the-Pooh to a very muddy place, and Pooh rolled about in the mud until he was black all over.

"Nobody would recognize me now, would they?" said Pooh.

"Why did you do that, Pooh?" Christopher Robin asked.

"So as to look like a little black cloud," said Pooh. "I want the bees to think I'm a little black raincloud, and that will deceive them."

"Silly old bear!" said Christopher Robin.

"Now," said Pooh, "give me the balloon back, please."

Four, three, two, one – and up went Pooh into the air, holding on to the balloon.

"Hold tight!" shouted Christopher Robin.

But Pooh couldn't hear him any more. He was singing another little song. He wanted to make the bees feel sure he really *was* a raincloud, so he was telling them so. The song went like this:

"I'm just a little black raincloud,
Hovering under your honey tree.
Only a little black raincloud.
Pay no attention to me."

And then Pooh went on, singing very quietly:

"You know a hungry old Pooh-cloud
Never gets hungry, no, not at all!
I'm just fooling around
Over the ground,
Wondering where I will fall."

Pooh liked his new song very much. He sang another verse of it.

"I'm not a hungry old Pooh Bear
I'm just a little black honey-cloud.
No one knows better than me, bees,
Stealing your honey is not allowed.
Everyone knows that a raincloud

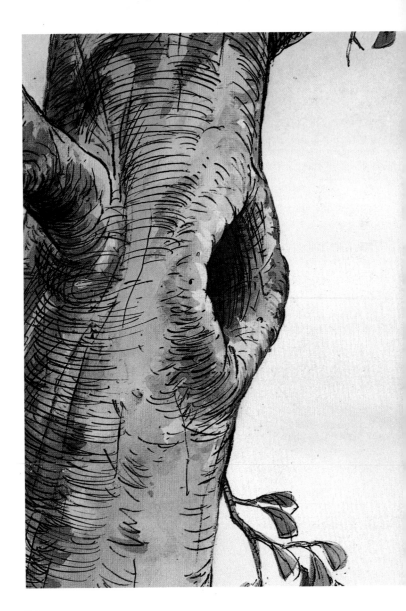

Never eats honey, no, not a nip!
I'm just floating around
Over the ground,
Wondering where I will drip!"

Pooh thought this was a very good song.
"And it's sure to deceive the bees!" he said to
himself.

But the bees must have noticed something,
because they began humming very loud, and in a
very excited way. Perhaps it was the singing that
excited them.
"Christopher Robin!" Pooh called down. "I
think these bees *suspect* something!"
"Perhaps they've noticed you're after their
honey, Pooh!"
"I'm just a little black raincloud," Pooh went on
singing bravely.

"I say, Christopher Robin! Perhaps *you* could help me deceive the bees!" said Pooh. "Could

you put your umbrella up and say, 'Tut, tut, it looks like rain!' "

"I say, Christopher Robin!" Pooh added, a little later. "I think these are the wrong *sort* of bees. Quite the wrong sort! I want to come down again. . . I . . .help! What's happening? The balloon is going down!"

Christopher Robin had shot a little hole in the balloon with his gun, so the air was going out of it – it really *was* going down, and so was Pooh.

"Help, Christopher Robin!"

"It's all right," said Christopher Robin. "I'll catch you, Pooh. There – that will teach you not to meddle with bees!"

But Pooh was not the bear to give in easily. If he wanted to eat honey, he was going to get some. The bees were buzzing and flying about in a threatening way, coming after him. "Thief!" they buzzed. "Thief! Trying to steal our honey! You watch out!"

Christopher Robin was just in time to put his umbrella up. He seized Pooh and jumped into the muddy puddle with him.

They sat there under the umbrella, quite safe from the bees

Pooh was glad to be back in the puddle again. He liked playing in the mud.

The bees swarmed about for a little longer, buzzing angrily. But they couldn't find Pooh and Christopher Robin under the umbrella.

Just think what they looked like when they came out of the muddy place – *two* little black rainclouds! It took both of them a long time to wash themselves clean again.

By now there was a terrible rumbling in Pooh's tummy. He had had a very dangerous adventure, and there still wasn't a drop of honey inside him! He looked inside his honey pots again, just in passing.

"Oh, look, Christopher Robin!" he cried.

"There's honey in my pots, real honey! Did *you* put it in them for me?"

"Yes, you greedy old bear!" said Christopher Robin.

And Pooh ate and ate and ate until he was full of honey.

Pooh felt happy. And sticky. And so he began to sing another song at the top of his voice.

It went something like this:

"Winnie-the-Pooh, Winnie-the-Pooh!
Tubby little cubby all stuffed with fluff!
I'm Winnie-the-Pooh, Winnie-the-Pooh!
Willy-nilly silly old Bear!"

Well, that was the story of Pooh and the Honey tree. I'll introduce you to some of my other friends in the next books. There's Eeyore, and Tigger and Rabbit, not forgetting Owl, and of course Kanga and Roo as well. And there's Piglet, Pooh's great friend.
I'm Christopher Robin, and when I got to know Pooh I was quite little, just seven years old. All my stories are true – as true as there's a Forest and a Hundred Acre Wood in it.